OBSESSED

WHISKEY RUN 3

HOPE FORD

Obsessed © 2021 by Hope Ford

Editor: Kasi Alexander

Cover Design: Cormar Covers

All rights reserved.

EVAN

I STAND IN THE CENTER OF THE McCARTHY Security office, surrounded by office equipment. The tiny whine of the printer, the refrigerator in the break room, and the fan on the ceiling seem much louder than they actually are. But I'm still getting used to this. I'm used to working in an office instead of at base, out in the open, with ten pounds of gear and a gun on my hip.

One month and three days. That's how long it's been since I was honorably discharged from the United States Army. All it took was one bad fall over six months ago to change my life forever. I had a concussion, but the doctors said I would be back at it in just a few weeks. No one can explain or in turn fix the extreme vertigo I started to experience. No matter what I tried, it didn't work. Numerous doctors, physical therapists, medicines and even

MRIs that showed nothing–nothing could explain why I had it or how to stop it. Yes, they finally found a medicine that helped it and made the symptoms more tolerable, but not enough that I could stay on active duty. Let's face it, no one wants a man with sudden bouts of dizziness and nausea to be the one having another person's back. No, I understand that. But it didn't make it any easier. Being in the service was my dream. Ever since I was little, playing army men, I knew what I wanted to be when I grew up. A badass willing to die for his country.

But my dream died one month and three days ago. I was discharged. Honorably, but still discharged. So I moved back home to Whiskey Run. Bought a fixer upper and started working with my brother in our family's security business. It's been in our family for generations, and even when we were little, our dad had us by his side, doing security and installations. It's second nature for me, and I stepped back into the role easily. I miss the activity and excitement, but I have to admit it's nice being back in Whiskey Run. It's changed a lot in the four years that I was gone. It seems it's more of a tourist town now with the way people come to tour the distillery and sample the Blaze Whiskey – which is what Whiskey Run is now famous for.

"Hey, you free to do a quote over at Red's Diner?"

My brother Sam interrupts my thoughts, and I nod in agreement without even thinking about it. I've discovered since I got back home, I do way better if I stay busy. Of course my idea of staying busy has been working in the office and away from the public, but I know I can't stay like this. I'm going to have to go out and work eventually. "Yes, sure."

Sam is writing on the white erase board all of the day's jobs with his back to me. "Good. Violet says she hasn't seen you since you got back so I told her I'd see if you were free."

"So she's taken over the diner now?"

"Yep, since her parents moved to Florida and retired. Around three years ago, I guess. Anyway, you'll be surprised when you see the place. She's made a lot of changes... good ones, though."

I feel like I've known Violet my whole life, and I feel a little guilty that I haven't gone in to see her yet. She's ten years older than me and the same age as Sam, but even with the age difference, I still would call her a friend. I can't explain why I've avoided people and places since I got back, but I have. Maybe I don't want the curious or pitying looks, and sure enough, if I go to Red's Diner where almost everyone in town eats at least once a week, that's exactly what I'll get. But I can't hide forever.

"Yeah, I'll go. I should have already gone in to

see Violet anyway," I tell Sam, and even I can hear the guilt in my voice.

He keeps flipping through the pages of his notepad and writing on the board as he mutters, "That's what she said."

"So what is she looking for? Did she say?"

He flips a few more pages. "Yeah. She needs her alarm updated for the front and back doors, and she's wanting to add a digital camera so she can access it from her phone."

"Great. Easy enough. I'll head over shortly."

I grab my notebook off the table and am about to walk into the supply room when Sam stops me. "Hey Evan, I know it's going to take you awhile to get adjusted to this, but I want you to know I'm glad you're home." He fans his hands around the office, but I know he's talking about more than just the office. He's talking about all of it—moving back home, leaving the Army, joining the family business.

"I know, Sam. Thanks for taking it easy on me this past month. I'm going to start earning my keep. And I'm glad to be back home too."

He nods, but it's obvious by the skeptical look in his eyes that he doesn't fully believe me. Hell, I don't either. But what choice do I have? I don't have one. So I'm going to make the best of it starting today.

Sierra

I blow out a breath as I stare out the window of the Whiskey Run Public Library. If I stand in a certain corner, slide halfway behind a bookshelf, and look to the corner of Main Street and Bruce Street, I can see the front door to McCarthy Security. Evan McCarthy is home. I knew as soon as he got here. I was at Red's eating lunch with Violet when a woman came from the hair salon saying she'd heard that Evan McCarthy was back in town and this time for good. She didn't have all the details except that he was honorably discharged from the army and was going back to work at his family's security firm.

Everyone was abuzz, excited that our town hero was home, but all I could do was worry. I knew that Evan had planned on being a lifer. He had no intentions of ever leaving the army, so the fact that he's home made me more than worried about him. Not that I could let him know. No, I would have to talk to him to do that. And that's one thing I don't do. I don't talk to Evan McCarthy. I may have watched him all growing up, I may have even helped him in English class a time or two. But that's it. We were exact opposites in high school, and he barely knew I existed.

From that day one month ago, I have spent more time at the front window of the library looking out, just hoping for a glance of Evan McCarthy. He's laid low since he got back, and the buzz of him being here has started to die down. No one talks about it anymore. Well, no one but me. I've never hidden the fact from Violet that I've had a crush on Evan since we were in high school together. Violet, who was in school with his older brother and in turn friends with him, has done everything to encourage me, even making me feel in small part there's a chance. She insists he would be crazy not to give me a chance. But then I'll leave from our book club meeting where we talk about books and gossip, and reality sets in. I'm the book nerd, the town librarian. I like order and planning. Evan was the star quarterback in high school. He dated the head cheerleader and was always with the in crowd. I assume he hasn't changed that much since graduating, and so I know I'm way out of my league.

Before I let the thoughts drown me, I remember how far I've come. I've quit comparing myself to others. I've quit being insecure about my weight, and I've learned to love the person I am. I've accepted that I'm socially awkward and most usually say the wrong thing. I'm me, and that's all I need to be. But now that Evan's back, I can sense my old insecurities coming back, and I want to kick myself for it. The stuttering, quiet girl that used to hide her eyes in a book all the time is rearing to come back, and I refuse to go back to the insecure, self-conscious woman that I used to be.

On that note, I gather the books that Violet requested and put them in a bag over my shoulder. I'm looking forward to delivering her books, having a slice of her famous cake, and catching up with one of my closest friends.

I make a point when I walk out of the library not to even glance over at the security firm. No, that's a dream I need to give up on. I keep my head pointed in the opposite direction with my shoulders squared. I look as if I'm ready to take on the world... now if only I felt like it too.

Red's Diner is only a block away. When I walk in, Violet is wiping off the counter, and she smiles when she sees me. The closer I get, the more it looks as if something is on her mind, something she's worried about. One thing I've learned about Violet is she's a very private person. I found out she was married, by accident really, but I've never met her husband, and even though I'd never gossip to anyone about my friend, I still wonder how she was able to get married and no one knows about it. So instead of asking her, I lift the bag off my shoulder to show her the books I'd brought. "Hey, Vi! I have those books you wanted."

Violet gestures to the almost empty diner. "Thank you. I didn't think I would be able to make it over there today, so I really appreciate you bringing them." I don't question her, though. I'm happy to come see her and chat.

I pull out one of the books and wiggle my eyebrows at her. It's a romance with a naked man chest on the cover.

She laughs and steals the book from my hand. "Look, don't judge me. You know romance books are my guilty pleasure."

I can't stop smiling. That's one of the things that actually got Violet and me talking at first. "Oh, I know. That's actually one of my favorite books."

We laugh conspiratorially, and then I sit down at the counter. "So what do I get for bringing you books? A piece of cake, a shake, what are you offering?"

"Whatever you want," she says.

I'm staring at the cakes on the counter. "Cinnamon Blaze apple cake. You know I can't pass it up. And a coffee."

Violet grabs me a slice of cake and a cup of coffee and sets it down in front of me. "So how are things at the library?"

"Quiet," I deadpan and then start heartily laughing at my own joke. I've learned to hide my quirky sense of humor from a lot of people, but Violet never judges me, and she's the one person I can truly be myself around.

"Hey, Violet." A man interrupts us, and I sober up quickly.

I turn my head so fast, I almost get dizzy. But there's no doubt in my mind who that voice belongs to. "Evan McCarthy," I breathe out low.

When he turns to look at me, I suck in a breath because it's then I realize that I said that out loud.

He stops next to me, shaking his head with his eyes scrunched up. "I'm sorry. Do I know you?" he asks.

My heart plummets in my chest. The man I've been pretty much been in love with almost half my life doesn't even have a clue who I am. If that's not a reality check, I don't know what is. "No." I shake my head, avoiding looking into his eyes. I could stand here all day looking at him. He hasn't changed a lot in the four years since I'd seen him. He's bigger. His shoulders are broader, his face more chiseled. But before I make an even bigger fool of myself, I look over at Violet, who's staring at me with sympathy. "Look, I have to get back to work, Violet. I'll see you soon, okay?"

I don't wait for her to respond. I grab my now empty bag and rush from the diner, not daring to look back.

2

EVAN

THE WOMAN COULDN'T GET OUT OF HERE FAST enough. I watch her all the way to the door before I turn to Violet. "What did I do?"

"You didn't do anything," Violet says, but I don't believe her. "I'm glad you're home, Evan."

I nod. "Yeah, me too. I'm sorry..." I start to apologize for just now coming to see her, but she waves me off.

"So a new security system. Can you help me out?"

I hold my hands up. I should just let it go, but the image of the stranger's retreating form is still in my head. "Wait. Who was that? She looks familiar, but I swear I can't place her."

Violet takes a deep breath. "That's Sierra Jensen. She went to..."

I interrupt her. "High school with me. That's

10

Sierra? The skinny girl with glasses and braces and her face always in a book?"

Violet winces at my description. "Yeah, that's the one. My friend that's smart and beautiful. The youngest librarian ever hired in Whiskey Run," she adds.

As if just realizing what I said and how it sounded, I start to backtrack. "I didn't mean..."

But Violet waves me off. "I know you didn't. It was a long time ago."

"She was always nice to me. Helped me in English. I wouldn't have passed Mrs. Rigsby's class without her."

"That's Sierra for you. She'll help anyone." She shakes her head with her forehead creased. "So can you look around and give me a quote on what I need?"

I keep looking toward the door, thinking that Sierra might come back. It looks like she left her cake and her coffee, but I nod at Violet. "Yeah, give me a few minutes. I'll take a look around and get out of your hair."

"No rush. It's a while before we get busy."

I walk away. Doing the quote is going to be easy, but I still want to see how dated her current equipment is. I do my job, but the whole time I'm thinking about Sierra and her reaction to me. The soft almost breathless way she said my name is still replaying in my head. Did she leave the way she did because I didn't recognize her? Was I mean to her in high school and not remember it? Why did she just leave like that? If I'd given it more time before opening my mouth I would have made the connection to who she is. The truth is, she has changed a lot since high school. She was pretty then, in a plain way. She always had a quiet way she carried herself, and I noticed her more than once. But back then, I knew someone as smart as her wouldn't have anything to do with a jock like me.

Once I'm finished taking notes, I go back to the counter where Violet is boxing up the cake and pouring fresh coffee into a to go cup. "I'll put together a quote later today and drop it off to you."

"Sounds good." She smiles at me, but it doesn't quite reach her eyes.

I'm about to turn and go but stop, remembering one of the things I need to talk to Violet about. "Hey, I never did thank you. While I was in the service, I received all the food and treats from the Whiskey Run Homecoming Committee. I know you had something to do with that, and I just want you to know I really appreciate it. It meant a lot to have a taste of home while I was gone."

But she shakes her head with a smirk on her face. "That wasn't me."

I stutter, embarrassed. "Oh, I just thought...."

"No, that was Sierra that did that. She sent the care packages out to you every week."

"Sierra." I say her name real slow. Sierra, the woman I was just rude to. She's the one that sent me a package every week. The one thing I looked forward to each week. Not only did she put in cookies and treats, she put in writing paper and pens, but she also always wrote a very sweet note thanking me for my service and that she hoped I was doing okay. But instead of signing it with her name, she always signed it *Whiskey Run Homecoming Committee.*

Violet is nodding her head as I make the connection. I lean on the counter. "Where did you say she worked?"

She gives me an inkling of a smile but then tries to hide it. I don't have time to ask her about it before she's answering my question. "I didn't. She works at the library. That's actually where I'm going now. She left her cake, so I was going to take it to her. I'll be sure to tell her you enjoyed the packages she sent."

She starts to walk past me, and I move in front of her, taking the bag and cup of coffee from her hands. "Wait. I'll take it. I need to thank her myself, I think."

Violet shrugs and hands over the items. "Sure. Thanks, Evan. It's good to have you back."

For the first time since I walked in, I give her a genuine smile. "Yeah, it's good to be back."

13

Sierra

WHAT WAS I THINKING? Did I really expect him to come back into town, see me, and just what—fall in love with me? I berate myself the whole way back to the library. I thought I was prepared. I could have made a joke about me helping him with English in high school or something like that. But instead I moaned out his name like he was touching me in my most private parts instead of just running into some guy I used to know in high school. My hand goes straight to my forehead. Oh my God, how embarrassing.

I make it back to the library in record time. I still have plenty of time left on my lunch break, but instead of sitting and reflecting on my embarrassment, I grab the book cart and start putting the books back on the shelves. Before I know it, twenty minutes have gone by, and my face is still heated just thinking about Evan.

My coworker is on lunch now, and when I hear the bells over the front door jingle, I walk out from the middle of the science fiction and fantasy section to see who it is. As soon as I spot Evan walking in, I jump back into place behind the shelves. Surely he didn't see me. What is he even doing here? I rest my head on the shelf in front of me. Can this day get any worse?

Since I'm the only one working, I know I'm going to have to go back out there and see what he wants. I guess my time for being mortified is not over yet. I suck in a deep breath, then another one, pull my shoulders back, and walk out from behind the shelves again. I slowly walk to the counter where he's standing.

Determined not to say his name again because who knows if I'm going to moan it again or what, I ask, "Can I help you find something?"

He holds out the cup and the bag in his hand. "Hey, Sierra. Violet was going to bring these to you, but I offered to do it. I hope that's okay."

I don't have any choice. I'll just make a scene if I turn down the things he brought. "Yes, of course, that was so nice of her... and you for bringing it. Thank you."

I take the Styrofoam containers from him and walk around the back of the counter. I need to put space between us, that's for sure. I set them down on the counter and clear my throat. "So yeah, uh, thank you again." And I force myself not to say anything more. Why is it I can't talk to him like a normal person?

"Yeah, you're welcome. I'm sorry I didn't recognize you, but you don't look anything like you did in high school."

This time, there's no way I can keep my face guarded because his words sting. I'm no longer the tiny girl I was in high school. Yes, I've gained weight, and obviously that's the first thing he's noticed. I hold up the bag that I'm sure has the cake in it. "Uh, yeah, I just can't seem to turn down the cake. So I need to get back to work."

I don't even wait for him to respond. I turn my back to him and grab some books off the shelf behind me. I walk back around the counter and away from him, hoping he gets the hint and leaves.

3

EVAN

I'M SO STUPID. THAT'S THE ONLY EXCUSE I HAVE. I'm used to dealing with the hard-edged men and women I served with. Obviously, I shouldn't be out in public. Even though I went there with an apology in mind and to thank her for the care packages, I totally screwed that up. When I made the stupid remark about not looking anything like she did in high school, I meant it as a compliment even though now, I realize it would have been an offhanded one at that. But before I could right my wrong, I saw the tears well up in her eyes and the way she wanted far from me. There's no way I was going to follow her and make an even bigger mess of it.

So what do I do? I tuck my head and walk back across the street to the office.

"How'd it go?" Sam asks.

17

"You don't want to know." I shake my head, remembering too late that he wasn't asking about Sierra, he was asking about the quote for Violet. "I mean the quote is fine. I'll drop it off this afternoon. Pretty cut and dried."

I walk past him and drop into the desk next to his.

Sam is watching me, no doubt wondering if he should ask me what's wrong or not. He's been walking on eggshells ever since I got back, and even though I probably need to talk to someone about Sierra, I'm not ready to yet. I'm not entirely sure why I'm so upset about the whole situation. It's not like I did anything wrong, really. But the fact I hurt her, even without meaning to, is weighing heavily on me. "I don't want to talk about it," I tell him before he decides to ask me about it.

Sam blows out a breath. "Okay then. Well, we got a call from the city while you were out. They are wanting to update the security cameras in their city operated buildings."

I sit up, paying more attention now. "Like the library? When do we start?"

His forehead creases. "Yeah, the library, the courthouse, city hall, the civic center... and we start tomorrow."

"I want the library," I tell him, not even considering beating around the bush. I have to find a way to talk to Sierra, make things right.

Sam has the gall to laugh. "Ahh, so you've seen Sierra, I take it?"

My whole body tenses up. Surely my older brother doesn't have a thing for the pretty librarian. If he does, I'll be nipping that in the bud. "What do you know about Sierra?"

He crosses his arms over his chest with a smirk. "Like you don't know?"

Really confused now, I ask, "Know what?"

He shakes his head. "Well, let's see, where do I start? She's liked you since high school..."

"She has not!"

He barks a laugh that echoes in the room and then rolls his eyes. "Yeah, you're right. She was a nerd—"

"Hey!" I say, instantly taking offense to that.

He shakes his head. "There's nothing wrong with it. But even knowing that, she came to every one of your games and couldn't take her eyes off you. She started coming around the house, helping Mom in the garden, talking to her about books. I mean, hello. She's sent you care packages for the last four years."

My mind starts to race. I don't remember her coming over to the house. "She was never at our house."

"All. The. Time. She would sit and wait, just hoping to get a glimpse of you. I felt bad for her actually, but you were always at practices or hanging out with your girlfriend or your jock friends. You didn't even notice her."

I get up and start pacing the room. Is he right? Did Sierra like me in high school? Is that why she sent the care packages with the sweet notes? I run my hand through my hair. Did I ruin any chance I have with her by opening my big, fat stupid mouth?

"The library... I'm starting it today."

He moves and stops in front of me. "The contract starts tomorrow."

I grit my teeth. "If they have a problem with it, I'll pay for it out of my own pocket. I'm starting it today."

He wants to argue with me, and I don't blame him. He's been the boss here since I left, and he's let me come in after four years away and be his partner. I'm probably pushing it, but I have to at least try and talk to Sierra today. If I go over there to apologize, she's going to run me off. But if I'm working on something that the city ordered to be done, she'll have no choice but to deal with me, and hopefully I can explain.

"Fine." Sam sighs, moving out of my way. "Just don't upset her. She's a good woman, Evan."

I nod but can't look him in the eye. I've already fucked it up and upset her earlier, but I'm going to make it right. I grab my equipment and head back across the street and into the library.

She's sitting behind the desk this time, and I

walk straight up to her. She pops up when she sees me, and it's obvious she's already looking around, wondering how she can get away from me. "Hey, Sierra."

She fidgets her hands in front of her but juts her chin at me. "Hello, Evan. Is there something I can help you with?"

I hold up my notebook, as if I have the contract in it when I don't. "Yeah, the city made an order for us to update the security equipment."

She breathes a sigh of relief. "Oh, okay. Well, I'll let you get to it then."

She's walking to the edge of her desk, and she's going to escape, I know she is, but I'm quicker than her. It's the quickest I've moved in a while. Since I started having vertigo I've had to really slow down my movements and be more intentional. But I'm not letting her escape.

She almost slams into my chest, and I drop the notebook so I can grab on to her shoulders to catch her. "Sorry, I didn't mean to startle you."

She nods but won't look up at me, and that's not going to do. I need her big brown eyes on me when I try to explain. "Sierra, look at me." I put a finger to her chin and tip it up.

Her eyes widen, and she looks frightened. I smile, doing my best to put her at ease. "We need to talk."

She blinks and continues to stare at me. At this

point, I'm not going to ask for more. "I owe you an apology for what I said earlier and for not remembering you when I first saw you."

She shakes her head. "No, it's fine, really. I'm pretty forgettable." She winces, and because I don't want to let her go, I put my hand on the side of her neck and rest it there. My thumb strokes right over her pulse, and it's practically vibrating under my touch.

"First of all, you're definitely not forgettable. I was a stupid kid... a dumb jock."

"You were not, you were smart."

I smile because even though she has every right to be mad at me right now and say some shit, she's still defending me. Maybe I haven't totally screwed up my chances. I take a deep breath. "No, if I was smart, I would have skipped the parties and instead I would have been hanging out with you."

She's shaking her head. No doubt nothing I'm saying to her makes sense.

"Thank you for sending me the care packages."

Shock registers on her face, and she pulls out of my grasp. "You're welcome. I just wanted you to know that we were thinking of you. I'm glad you're home and safe." Still she looks as if she's been caught. "I mean, I would have done it for anyone."

I nod, but we both know the truth. I decide right then that I can't just let this go. "Go out with me?"

She's already shaking her head. "No, that's not a good idea."

"Why not?"

She picks up books off the table and holds them to her chest. Her long black hair is in waves across her shoulders, and the way she's holding herself it's like she's trying to hide her face from me. "Because you feel bad for this morning. That's the only reason you're asking me out. I've forgiven you. It's done. Thank you, but no thank you." And this time I know the only way to stop her from leaving where I'm at is to physically stop her, and already I know I've lost some of her trust, so I'm not going to do that. I step to the side and watch her walk off.

Her pants are tight against her shapely curved ass, and I don't want to look away. How in the world did I ignore this woman in high school? How did I find interest in anyone else when she was right under my nose?

I go to the back of the library and check the rear door, measuring and looking at the hardware already in place. It's an industrial door, and I'll have to bring more parts to do it, which is fine by me. It will give me an excuse to come and see her again tomorrow. I walk to the front of the library and install the camera, rewire the outlet, and update the code panel. When everything is ready, I call her to the front. She walks slowly toward me, no doubt worrying what I'm going to say next. I know I don't even have a chance to get close to her if she has her guard up with me all the time. "Hey, sorry to bother you, but I just wanted to go over the new alarm."

She nods and stands beside me to look at the panel. Her soft flower scent fills my nose. "Uh, you hit this button, then the code." I show her the numbers. "And then you hit the away button when you're leaving. If you are staying, you would then push stay instead of away."

She repeats everything I just said. When I nod my head, staring at her, trying to will her to look at me, she doesn't. She just says "thanks" and walks back to her desk.

I'm not used to being dismissed, but I can't be mad about it. "I'll be back in the morning to install the rear alarm."

She nods and starts helping someone else. Reluctantly, I walk away.

4

SIERRA

HE FEELS GUILTY. THAT'S ALL. THAT'S WHY HE asked me out. I repeated that to myself all night last night and this morning as I walked into the library. I refuse to let myself get caught up in the past. At one time, all I could think about was Evan McCarthy. I refuse to fall into that trap again.

I've had to mentally prepare myself all morning knowing that I'm going to see him today when he comes to finish the alarm system. I barely get to the front of the library when I can feel his eyes on me. "Morning, Sierra."

I plan to only glance his way, but the smile on his face and the way the blue of his shirt brings out the blue of his eyes gets me all messed up. I trip over my own feet, and I prepare to fall through the glass door of the library, clenching my eyes tightly shut. Before I can hurt myself, Evan's strong arms go around me, and he pulls me tight against his body.

He doesn't let go. He stands there with his arms tight around me. "That's twice I've almost caused you to fall, but I'm not going to lie to you, I like the way you end up in my arms."

My hands go to his chest, and I mean to push away, but what do I do? I curl my fingers into the front of his shirt and hold on tight. I'm staring up at him, completely lost in his gaze and speechless. His lips are so close to mine, I could just raise up an inch on my tiptoes, pull him down by his collar, and kiss him.

His hands tighten on my waist. "I would like to kiss you right now, but I'm guessing you don't want Cassie over at Sugar Glaze to tell the town that I'm violating you in front of the library."

I reluctantly drag my eyes from his and look down the block, and sure enough, Cassie is standing outside the bakery watching us. I step out of Evan's embrace, and for the briefest of seconds, he hesitates on letting me go. He could have kissed me and I wouldn't have tried to stop him. As a matter of fact, there's no way I would have been able to stop him.

I turn quickly and pull my purse off my shoulder to dig out the keys while Evan picks up his papers he dropped on the ground. I walk into the library, the buzzing of the alarm sounding. I have thirty seconds to put the code in, and I'm drawing a blank, staring at the panel. Evan comes up behind me, his front to my back, and reaches around to punch in the code.

I mumble "thanks," slide under his arm, and go to my desk. My resolve to stay away from Evan McCarthy is weakening, and I know I need to put some space between us. I gather some books to start putting them away, ignoring him. Eventually, he goes to the back without another word. He works in the back, and I get lost in straightening the library. I love the mornings at the library. It's the least busy time, and usually when I get everything set up for the day, I'm able to peruse the aisles to find the next books I want to read.

Evan comes from the back, and I do my best to look busy, but that doesn't stop him. "Hey, Sierra. I'm done with the back door."

I paste a smile to my face. "Great. Thanks for doing it."

He nods and walks toward me. "I just need you to sign here that the work is complete."

I take the pen from him, making sure I don't touch his fingers, and then sign my name.

I can feel his gaze boring into me, but I don't look up, I can't.

"Do you want me to show you how it works?"

Instantly, I shake my head side to side. "No, that's okay. It's the same as the front, right?"

"Yes, the very same, it just required a bigger panel and more wires."

I walk away while telling him, "All right, well you take care. It's good to see you home again."

I don't expect him to follow me, but he does. "Go out with me," he tells me. And then, as if realizing how bossy and demanding he sounds, his voice softens. "I mean, will you go out with me?"

I shake my head, eyes clenched before I finally peel them open and stare at him with sadness. "Please quit asking me. It's not a good idea, you and me."

He takes a step toward me. "Yes, it is."

I take a step back, holding a hand up to stop him from advancing. "No, it's not. Please quit asking me."

Evan

I WAIT for a hint that she's weakening, but her face is guarded, telling me nothing. Could I have had it wrong? Maybe she sent the care packages for the reason she said. Maybe she would do it for just anyone. Maybe I'm not special to her at all.

I clasp my mouth shut and with one last glance, I walk away. I don't plan to give up, but obviously what I have going on is not working. I get almost to the door when she calls out my name, and I spin on foot so fast I almost lose my balance. The vertigo strikes, but luckily there's a tall sturdy bookshelf next to me, and I reach out to grab on to it. My eyes close, and the room starts to spin. I don't open my eyes, but I can hear her feet pounding on the hardwood floor as she runs to me. Her hands go to my waist. "Evan. Evan. Are you all right?"

I leave one hand on the shelf, but the other goes to her shoulder. I want to look at her, but I'm afraid to open my eyes. Sometimes it makes it worse, and sometimes it helps. All I know is when it's worse, nausea rolls in my stomach, and I definitely don't want to throw up here in her library.

She holds me tighter. "Evan, talk to me. What do I need to do? Do you have your pills?"

I nod and reach for the front of my jean pockets, but my hand is shaking so bad finally she moves my hand and digs into my pocket, pulling the small bottle out. "How many?"

"One," I moan.

"Let me get you some water." She's about to let go, but my other hand goes to her shoulder to hold her still. I chance a peek at her and open my eyes into small little slits. "I can take it without."

She puts the tiny pill into my hand, and I take it quickly.

We stand there just like that, and I'm kicking myself for letting her see me like this. "I gotta go."

She grabs on to my shirt and pulls me over to a table, pulls the chair out by hooking her foot around the leg and then helps me sit down. "You aren't going anywhere. Not until I know you're okay."

"I'm fine," I mutter, tension thick in my voice. And then it hits me. She knew. She knew I was on a pill. She knew what was wrong with me.

"How did you know I have vertigo?"

Her face is stricken, as if she just got caught telling something she wasn't supposed to. But instead of apologizing, she tells me plainly, "Your brother told Violet, and I promise you that I'm the only person Violet has told."

"Fuck." I grunt, rubbing my hands across my face. I can't look at her. "So that's it, huh?"

Her hand goes to my knee, and I stare at her fingers with the pink on her tips. "What is it?"

I shrug. "That's why you didn't want to go out with me. You know I'm having issues and you know what, I don't blame you. It's fucked up."

She doesn't say anything for a minute, and finally I raise my eyes to hers. What I see is a surprise, though. I never dreamed she'd be mad. "Really, Evan McCarthy? Do I seem like a shallow, arrogant woman that wouldn't go out with a man because he has vertigo?" She shakes her head, and she doesn't even try to hide her disgust. "You don't know me at all."

"Sierra, I'm—"

But she don't even let me finish. "No, come on, I'm going to help you across the street and then I have to get to work."

I bristle and tell her between clenched teeth, "I don't need help across the street."

"Fine," she says, waving her hand, gesturing me to leave. If my head wasn't pounding, I'd stay, but I can't even think straight right now.

"Fine," I tell her as I walk past her with as much dignity as I can muster. I know her gaze follows me all the way across the street, down the block, and she doesn't look away until I walk into McCarthy Security.

"Damn, what's happened to you?" Sam asks as soon as I walk into the door.

I'm holding my head. "Nothing. I just need a few minutes. I had to take a pill. I should be good in fifteen to twenty minutes."

He doesn't question me, just nods his head, and I walk into the break room and sit back on the couch. I take deep, cleansing breaths and try to let my mind free.

After thirty minutes of sitting there, I finally feel like I can function again. I work the rest of the morning helping Sam prepare for the city office installations, scheduling out the rest of the week. I'm sitting at the conference table where I have a perfect view of the library. At lunch time, Sierra walks out and locks the door. She only gets a few steps from the door when a man walks up to her.

My jaw clenches. It looks innocent enough, but I don't like it. The man seems as if he's leaning into her. "Sam, who is that?"

Sam walks over and peeks out the window. "That's Jake. He and Sierra must have made up."

Made up? I stand up and crowd the window to watch where they go. I think I'm about to lose sight of them until they stop and hug, and she walks into Red's Diner. Fury is building inside me. I pace the room, ignoring the smirks I keep getting from my brother. I need to just lock this down. I know I can't force her to go out with me, but I need a plan.

5

SIERRA

I BARELY LET VIOLET PULL UP A CHAIR BEFORE I start blabbing. All morning after Evan left, I fought with myself on whether I should have followed him over to his office or not. He walked just fine, but maybe his ego was dented. And should I be pissed that he thought I cared about his vertigo – as if that would be a reason not to date someone. But just the fact he said it tells me a lot more about Evan than I already knew. He's hurting. There's no doubt about it. And then I find a letter in the night box at the library, and so I have that to worry about too.

"He asked me out."

Violet smirks. "Who did?"

I roll my eyes. She knows exactly who I'm talking about. Besides books, Evan McCarthy is the only subject I ever talk about. "Evan."

She practically starts bouncing in her seat.

"That's so exciting! When are you going? Where are you going?"

I want to revel in her excitement. I want to be able to let myself go and be excited as she is, but I'm not. I can't let myself. "I told him no."

As soon as I say it, I sit back and wait for the wrath from Violet. I know it's coming. She sputters and stutters before finally getting it out. "But why? Why would you tell him no?"

I shrug, not wanting to get into it, but I know that won't fly with Violet. She sets her cup of coffee down on the table in front of her and leans toward me. "Sierra, you have been in love with Evan since high school."

I'm shaking my head. "I wouldn't call it love." I look up at the ceiling to avoid her all-knowing look. "A crush. I had a crush on him."

She snort-laughs, and I reach over to grab her hand because everyone in the restaurant is staring at us. "What? That's all it was. I'm over it."

Violet just continues to shake her head. "You can't just throw this away. A crush, love, whatever you want to call it, you don't just say no because you're scared."

I jut my chin out at her. "I'm not scared."

She nods her head, her eyes big. "Yes, you are. He's a good guy, Sierra. You know he is, I know he is. I know you, and you think it's pity or whatever, but it's not. You didn't see his face when he found out you were the one that sent him all the care packages. That meant a lot to him."

I'm quiet for so long I finally decide to change the subject. "So, when are you going to talk to me about your secret?"

She leans back in her chair. "I don't have any secrets."

It's my turn to snort. "Really? You mean the marriage certificate I found with your name on it... that's not a secret?"

"I don't want to talk about it," she says, and before I can ask her anything else about it, she changes the subject. "So what about you? You still feel like someone's watching you?"

Shoot. I almost let myself forget about it. For the past few months, weird things have been happening. I've felt like I've been watched a few times I swear that things have been moved around my house. But as soon as I get freaked out about it, days will go by with nothing, and I'll convince myself that everything is fine.

I dig into my purse and pull out an envelope and lay it on the table between us. "I found this in the night drop."

She reaches out and picks it up gingerly, as if she's waiting for a bomb to go off. Slowly, she opens it and unfolds the paper and reads it. I already have the message committed to memory and say it word for word with her. "Sierra, I've been out of town but don't worry I'm back. I missed you and I can't wait for the day that we are finally able to be together. I'll be seeing you soon my sweetheart. With love, X."

She trembles, and it's the exact same way I reacted when I read it.

She holds the paper up. "You have to call the police."

I nod. She's been trying to tell me that for a while, but this is the first true account that someone is following me. "I know, you're right."

She points at me. "You hesitated. Why did you hesitate?"

I shrug my shoulders. "What if it's just some harmless situation? I don't want to get anyone in trouble. I mean, he hasn't done anything wrong."

Violet grabs my hand. "But it can be. You don't know, that's the whole point. You should tell Evan. He'd know what to do."

I'm already shaking my head when I hear, "Tell me what?"

I gasp and look at the big man looming over us. How in the world he snuck in without either of us knowing is beyond me. "Evan!" I say as if I've been caught red-handed.

Evan

I WALK in and Violet and Sierra are in deep conversation. When I get close, I hear my name and they both look up in shock at me when I say, "Tell me what?"

Violet slides across the booth and stands up, gesturing for me to sit down. She doesn't say anything to me; instead she points at the piece of paper on the table and tells Sierra, "You should tell him, Sierra. He can help."

But Violet is already shaking her head as she reaches for the paper. Luckily, I'm faster than her, grab it up and scan the message while I sit down across from her. When I'm done, I hold it up. "What is this? Who gave this to you?"

She clasps her hands on the table in front of her while I try to contain the fury that is surging through my veins. "I found it in the night return box at the library."

"Who is it? Who is X?"

She lifts her shoulders and sighs. "I don't know. Uh, but actually I was going to go and talk to Sam about putting in an alarm system at my house."

My fists clench on the table, wadding the paper in my hands. "Has this guy been to your house?"

She flinches. "Uh, well, I'm pretty sure someone has, but I can't prove it. Just things moved around, things like that. I'm sure it's nothing; I just thought a security system will make me feel safer, ya know. Is Sam at the office? Maybe I can stop by and talk to him about it before my lunch break is over."

"I'll do it," I tell her.

"Under the circumstances, it's probably better if I get Sam to do it."

I lean back in the booth, crossing my arms on my chest. "Because I have vertigo?"

She throws her hands up in the air. "No, God, not because you have vertigo. I don't care that you have vertigo." Her face is flushed. "I mean, I care, but not for the reasons you think they are. You are a perfectly capable man. I mean because of my crush..."

I lean in then. "Go ahead. Finish it. Finish what you were going to say."

She blows a breath out. "Fine. It's not like you didn't know anyway. I made a fool of myself enough times because of it. I had a crush on you in high school. I just think it's better if we stay..."

I stand up and walk around to her side of the table. I put one hand on the table in front of her and one on the booth behind her. I lean over until she's so close that her sweet scent hits my nose. I inhale deeply, not even caring if she knows I'm smelling her. "I have a crush on you, Sierra. Today. Right now. And I'm pretty sure it could be more. So what we're going to do is we're going to take this to the police station and give a report. I'm going to check the security cameras for the library and see who put that in the box last night, and then when you get off work, I'm going to your house to install your alarm."

She's looking up at me, her eyes wide. "Then what?"

And fuck if the way she says it doesn't make my balls clinch. "Then I'm going to kiss you."

6

SIERRA

I can't believe I agreed to this. I'm driving my little Honda away from downtown toward my house. I keep looking in the rearview mirror, and Evan's right behind me. He did exactly what he said he'd do: He went with me to the police station and sat with me while I explained all the weird things that have been happening, and then I gave them the letter. They made a report, but unfortunately that's about all they can do at this point. However, Evan made them promise to patrol my neighborhood more, so there's that at least. He then walked me to the library and programmed his number into my phone. "I'll be right across the street. Don't go anywhere without me." He was bossy and demanding and normally I'd get upset about being told what to do, but the way he said it had me just nodding my head at him.

And now, here we are, pulling into my driveway and when he parks next to me, I get out to meet him. "Did you check the library cameras? Could you tell who dropped the letter?"

He gathers up equipment from the back of his truck and meets me at my steps. "No, whoever it was had a hat pulled down real low on his face. I made a copy of it and gave it to the police."

"Okay," I tell him before leading him inside. I had hoped he would find out who it was and it would be over with, but apparently that's not going to be the case.

He's looking around my small but cozy living room. "I like your house."

I feel pride looking around. I had to save for a long time to get this house, and even though it's small, it's mine. "Thank you." I walk a few feet away. "I'll be in the kitchen if you need anything. Do you want a soda or water? I may have a beer."

"No thanks." He gets to work, and instead of the usual flirting, he seems to be all business. I could curl up on the couch and just watch him work, but I know that would be weird. So instead I go to the kitchen and see what I can fix for dinner. I get lost in cooking when I turn at a noise. Evan is leaning against the doorway, watching me work.

"Hey, are you done already?"

He nods. "Something smells good. I missed lunch today."

I know he's hinting, and I figure it's the least I can do. "Do you want to stay for dinner?"

He walks into the room, and I turn back to the stove. He's hovering over me, and I can feel the heat from his body at my back. "Mmmmmm. Spaghetti. It's my favorite."

I plate the food and slide away from him and set it down on the table. "Have a seat."

He sits down, and I grab drinks and silverware before sitting across from him.

He takes a bite and moans around the mouthful. "This is good."

My face heats. "Thanks. So I've been meaning to ask, you okay after this morning?" I'm worried that I may have brought up a sore subject, but I've been worried about him all afternoon.

"Yeah, I'm good actually. I called my doctor, and there's a new drug that just came out. He said I needed to get on it, so he called it in, and Sam went and picked it up for me. I took it this afternoon and already I feel like a new man. Or well, the same man before I started having vertigo."

"Oh, Evan. That's great! I'm so happy for you."

He stares at me, and his gaze is heated as he tells me thanks.

"So uh, how's it been being back?"

He shrugs. "I sort of avoided everyone the first month I got back, just trying to get my feet under me. I'm doing good now. I saw a girl I knew in high school, and she's pretty much all I've been thinking about lately."

Jealousy surges until I look up at him and there's a twinkle in his eyes. He must be able to read my expression. "You, Sierra. I'm talking about you."

Pleasure hits me in the chest, but I still can't trust it.

"Go out with me? To a movie and dinner?"

Before he even finishes his sentence, I'm shaking my head. "No."

He huffs, dropping his fork on his already empty plate. "Do you want more?" I ask him, and when he shakes his head, I grab both of our plates and take them to the kitchen. He follows right behind me. "Why? Why won't you go out with me?"

I turn on the hot water and start washing dishes. He grabs a towel off the hook and stands next to me, gesturing for me to hand him the clean dish in my hands.

I hand it over and decide I'm going to be honest with him. "Because you're just going to hurt me."

"Hurt you? I'd never hurt you," he says fiercely.

I turn to the side and put one hand on my hip. "Look at you and then look at me. We're different. Too different. You were the prom king. You dated the head cheerleader. The sooner that I get you out of my head, the better off I'll be."

I go to turn back toward the sink, and he stops me. "Sierra, we're not in high school anymore."

When I don't respond, he asks, "Was I mean to you in high school?"

I shake my head. "No. Never."

"Have I given you any indication that all I want from you is sex?"

My face flushes. "No," I squeak. "But you're just back in town. I'm sure you haven't heard yet, but Jessica and her husband are getting divorced."

He shakes his head, confused. "Jessica? Who's Jessica?"

I barely resist rolling my eyes. "Your prom date."

He laughs. "Are you kidding me right now? I'm not interested in Jessica or anyone else that you want to match me up with. I'm interested in you."

"I..." I start to tell him I can't, but he leans down until we're nose to nose.

"I want to kiss you, Sierra."

Because I'm weak, I nod my head, and he smiles at me. He leans in, and his lips briefly touch mine before he pulls away. I go up on my tiptoes to follow him, and his smile gets even bigger. His hand goes to the nape of my neck, and I angle my head to the side. His lips cover mine, but instead of a peck this time, he devours me. His tongue mates with mine, and I wish right then for it never to end. My nipples harden, and there's a pull in my lower belly, an ache inside me that is building. And just when I'm sure I'm going to beg him to take me to the bedroom, I surprise both of us. "I can't."

He pulls back slowly. I don't know which one of us is more surprised.

"Let me show you the alarm system."

I follow behind him and stop next to the panel on the wall. He shows me everything and then downloads the app on my phone so I can see the yard and front door from the camera.

"Thank you for this. How much do I owe you?"

He shakes his head. "We'll send you an invoice."

I want to argue with him, but maybe that's how it works. It doesn't matter, I'll make sure I pay him. He interrupts my thoughts. "I know you think this isn't a big deal, but you need to be careful. If you see anything that worries you or is just odd, you call me or the police."

I'll call the police. I don't say it out loud, but that's my plan. The less time I spend with Evan the better. He may say he's interested in me, but I don't believe him.

"Okay."

He gathers his things and walks toward the door. "Is this because of Jake?"

My forehead creases. "Jake? What about Jake?"

"My brother said you and he must have made up. Are you seeing him?"

I laugh out loud. "Is that what he told you? Did

he tell you that I was mad at Jake because he got drunk at the last book club meeting?" He shakes his head.

"Okay. Did Sam tell you that Jake is gay?"

Evan shakes his head. "No, he didn't tell me that."

"Yeah, so I'm not dating Jake."

"Good," he says, perking up a little.

"Good?" I question him.

"Yeah, because that means there's not a man in my way." He leans down and kisses me on the lips before I catch on to what he's doing. "Not that a man would have mattered, Sierra. Because I've already made the decision that you're going to be mine."

"Yours!" I say loudly.

He gives me a cocky laugh. "That's right. Mine. When all is said and done, you're going to be mine."

He turns and walks away as my mouth falls open and I stare at him go. He stops at his truck. "Lock the door and turn on the alarm."

And he doesn't look away until I walk inside and shut the door, leaving me to wonder what I've gotten myself into.

7

EVAN

I GOT AS FAR AS THE END OF THE ROAD BEFORE I turned back around. There's something that stops me from leaving. I sit in my truck all night and watch the neighborhood. It has to be the quietest, most boring neighborhood in all of Whiskey Run. The most excitement all night was when Old Man Larry let his dog Squeaks out at two in the morning, and he went across the road, pooped in the neighbor's yard, and then came back.

That was it. I was sure it was safe to leave Sierra and go home, but I couldn't. So when the clock turns seven-thirty and I see Sierra walking out of her house with her head down, it's easy to get out of the truck and walk up to her. She doesn't even notice me until she's almost up on me.

She puts her hand over her chest. "Evan. You scared me to death."

She looks me up and down. "What are you doing here?" She looks at where my truck is parked. "Did you stay out here all night?" No doubt she's noticed I'm in the same clothes I had on yesterday.

I scrub my hand through my hair. "I did." I grab her hand and pull her with me. "C'mon, I'll take you to work."

She walks a few feet with me. "Wait, you stayed out here all night?" she asks in awe.

"I did. I need a shower, but first I'm going to make sure you get to work okay, have Sam keep an eye on you, and then I'll run home and shower."

She's going to argue with me, I know she is. Either about me staying out here all night or about me taking her to work, but I'm ready for it.

She finally starts walking toward the truck, and when I open the door for her she climbs in.

I get into the driver's seat and put the truck into gear. "You really slept out here all night?"

She's stunned, and I don't understand why. "Yeah, why wouldn't I?"

I peek over at her and she's looking at me incredulously. "Why would you?"

I've shocked her; that's probably the only reason she's letting me drive her to work. "Why would I? Uh, because I got to the end of the road and knew I couldn't leave. I wanted to make sure you were safe, and the only way to do that was to be outside your house in case you needed me."

48

"Evan," she says, and I wait for her to continue. "Evan, no one... I mean, well, I can't believe you did that... for me."

"I wasn't joking last night, Sierra. I meant what I said. I know you don't trust me or believe we could make a go of this. Heck, I can't even convince you to date me, but I don't plan on giving up."

She doesn't comment, and we ride the rest of the way in silence. I walk her to the entrance of the library and walk in with her, making sure everything is secure. I go down the line of everything she needs to do to be safe, to not leave without me, and to call if she needs anything.

"You're making a bigger deal of this than you should. It's probably nothing, and I feel bad that you've completely changed your life to deal with it." She says it in a quick jumble of words.

I ignore her as if she didn't say anything. "What about lunch? I can come by and take you somewhere or I can bring you something."

She points to one of the bags she just set down. "No, I brought it."

With her distracted, I move closer to her, and when she turns back to me, I kiss her quickly. "Okay, I'll be back at five, but promise to call me if you need anything."

She touches her fingers to her lips. "Okay."

With another glance at her, I walk out of the

library and across the street to the office. Luckily, I had a change of clothes in my truck, and I shower at the office. I work all day, and I discover that I'm obsessed. I pull up the feed of the library's security system, and I'm able to see her when she walks by the front windows. A few times through the day, I notice she's staring out onto the street, and I walk out of the security firm and look her way. As if caught, she waves and then slinks back behind a shelf. Was she looking for me?

My heart swells in my chest thinking that maybe she was.

At five o'clock, I'm picking her up and walking with her to the truck. "Anything out of the ordinary happen today?"

She shakes her head. "No, see, I told you we were making a bigger deal of this than we should."

I help her in and when I get in, she exclaims. "What is that smell?"

"I picked up pizza from Giovanni's. And a movie."

She folds her hands in her lap. "Are you inviting yourself to my house for dinner and a movie?"

I put the truck into gear and drive toward her house. "Well, if I can't get you to go out with me, then I guess I'm going to stay in with you."

She laughs, and I relax a little. She could've point blank told me no, but she didn't. Maybe I'm at least moving in the right direction and making her feel like she can start to trust me.

"I hate to ask, but do you care if we stop at the grocery store real quick? I'm out of coffee."

I gasp. "Out of coffee? Oh no."

She slaps me playfully as she laughs out loud. "You laugh now, but you haven't seen me without coffee."

I shiver like I'm scared, and she laughs again. I love seeing this relaxed side of her. I stop at the market that's on the way to her house, and she jumps out before I can get her door. "You don't have to go in if you don't want. I promise I'll be quick."

But I shake my head and grab on to her hand. "Take all the time you need."

She stumbles a little but catches herself. I wait for her to pull her hand away, but she doesn't. We walk straight to the coffee aisle, and she picks it out and starts to walk toward the front. "Wow, you weren't kidding. I figured you'd find something else you needed while you were in here."

"Nope. Just the coffee. I told you I'd be quick."

We're standing in line when I feel her tense next to me. I look around, trying to find a threat or what has her upset when I lean down in front of her. "What's wrong?"

But before she can answer, I hear it. A sing-song

voice from behind me. Sierra pulls her hand from mine. "Evan McCarthy, is that you? I heard you were back in town."

I roll my eyes at Sierra and turn around to face the woman from my past. And when I do, I put my arm around Sierra. "Hey, Jessica. How you doing?" That's right. The woman from my past, my prom date. What are the chances of running into her here?

She stands closer to me than I like, and I pull Sierra tighter under my arm. But Jessica doesn't seem to notice because she reaches out and touches my shoulder. "I'm doing good. Well, I'm getting divorced, but I'm sure you've heard. Maybe we can get together and catch up."

But I'm already shaking my head. "I'm sorry to hear about your divorce, but actually, I'm spending all my time with Sierra."

And it's then Jessica looks at Sierra as if noticing her for the first time. She then gives us a quick goodbye and walks toward the back of the store.

All the progress I thought I made with Sierra is now gone, because as soon as Jessica walks away, she pulls out from my arm. She's tense all the way to the truck, and she doesn't say a word until we pull into her driveway. "You know, you could have gone with her."

I blow out a breath. "Is that what this is about? I

have no interest in Jessica. I didn't even want to go out with her in high school. I did because it was expected of me. Now I do what I want. And I want to be with you."

She beams over at me, and for once I know I said the right thing.

Hours later I find that I wasn't prepared to sit next to her on the couch for hours and not touch her. We started off with a cushion between us, and slowly we moved and eventually met in the middle. We've long ago eaten the pizza and finished the first movie. Now, there's some reality TV show on, but neither of us is watching it. I've asked her twenty questions it seems like and with every answer she gives me, I find that we have way more in common than I initially thought. She loves to watch the History Channel, enjoys any action movie, and is hooked on Jeopardy.

We're laughing, and she's more relaxed now than she's ever been. I don't want to ruin it, but I don't think I can resist any longer. I put my hand on her shoulder. "I'm going to kiss you now."

Her eyes widen and dilate. Her tongue pokes out to wet her lips, and I hold in my groan as I lean in and kiss her. As soon as our lips touch, I hold her in my embrace. But that's not close enough. I pull her onto my lap and show her how I feel about her. If she's not going to listen to me, maybe she'll believe it if I show her. And there's no way she can not see how I feel about her by the way we mesh together. It's a perfect union, and when I eventually pull away, we're both breathless.

I lean my forehead to hers. "I better go, or I'm going to try and talk you into letting me stay."

She's about to do it. She's about to let me, but I don't want it this way. I don't want to pressure her. I want her to decide she wants me on her own.

"You can..." She starts, but I put my finger on her lips to stop her.

"Don't finish that. Before we get to that point, I need to know you trust me. And I can't believe I'm fucking saying this, but when I take you, Sierra, it's for keeps. I can't do it and you have second thoughts about it. We can wait, there's no rush."

I get up from my seat. The bulge in my pants is uncomfortable, but I'm not going to draw attention to it.

She follows behind me. "You're tired. And I know that is not good for your vertigo."

"Actually this new medicine has been great. I haven't had one symptom since yesterday."

"Oh, that's great news. But still, you need your rest. You can't sleep in your truck. Please go home and rest. I'll see you in town tomorrow."

I lean down and kiss her. "I'll be here to get you in the morning."

She's already shaking her head. "I can drive..."

I wrap my hand around the base of her neck. "I know you can, but I want to drive you. I like having you with me. Is that okay?"

She nods slowly, and I kiss her again. "Now, I better go. Lock the door and set the alarm."

She looks at me dreamily. "I promise."

It's then I decide to push my luck. "Go out with me."

I'm ready for the no. I'm sure she's going to say it but instead, she says, "Okay," and I can't resist. I kiss her again.

I step out the door and hear her set the alarm before I descend the steps. I'm just going to run home real quick, grab some clothes, shower, and then I'll be back to sit outside her house again. She's right, I'm tired, and besides the nap I had on the couch today at work, I've hardly slept. But I know I won't sleep if I'm across town, so I'm coming back.

I get out of the shower and pick up my phone to log into Sierra's security system. I've been on edge since I left her neighborhood, and so I decide I'll survey the place on my phone until I can get back to her.

I'm combing my hair when movement on my phone catches my eye. There's someone standing in her driveway. He's in the shadows, but sure as shit there's a man standing there. I hit the silent alarm button for her house, knowing the cops will be notified and on their way in an instant.

I pull on clothes and run outside to my truck. My tires squeal on the pavement as I speed across town, taking curves way too fast.

I'm dialing her number when an incoming call comes in, and her picture pops up on the ID.

"Sierra," I breathe into the phone. I want to talk to her, but I hate having eyes off her house.

"Evan, oh my God, there's someone outside my window. I started screaming, and he's knocking at my door."

She's absolutely terrified, and so am I. If anything happens to her, I won't forgive myself. I never should have left her. "I know. I saw it on the cameras. I'm on my way, and the police will be there soon."

She's breathing frantically into the phone, and it guts me knowing how scared she is and I'm not there to help her. "Sierra, listen to me. Go to your room and get in your closet. Don't answer the door for anyone. You only open the door when I get there. Do you understand?"

She's panting heavily, and I hear her tearing through her house. When there's an echo, I know she's in her closet. "I'm in here. I'm in my closet." Her voice has dropped to a whisper.

"Okay, keep talking to me. It's going to be okay, I'm almost there."

She screams, and I swear I lose ten years off my life. "What is it? What's happening?"

"There's someone pounding now. They're hollering police. Should I go open the door?"

"No! Do not open the door. I'm two blocks away. You open the door for me, that's it."

I push even harder on the gas, even though I already have it to the floor. I take the corner to her road on two wheels. There are blue lights in front of her house, and I get out, recognizing Officer Bales. "She won't answer the door."

"Honey, I'm here. Open the door."

Five seconds later, she has the front door open, and she's diving into my arms. Her legs go around me, and I'm holding her so tight I know I'm hurting her, but I can't let her go.

I turn to Officer Bales. "We'll be right back."

His gaze is on her ass, but he's nodding his head, and I turn real quick and slam the front door behind me. I stride across her living room, down the hall, and walk into her bedroom. She's still wrapped around me, and when I look at us in the floor length mirror across the room, I see what Jensen was looking at. Sierra has a T-shirt on, and the way she's hanging on to me, you can see her panty-clad ass plain as day. My head drops to her shoulder. *Fuck, Evan. Now is not the time. Get your shit together,* I tell myself.

"Honey, you need to get some clothes on, and

we're going to go out and see the policeman and see if they found the guy."

She's shaking her head. "Sierra, baby, you have to talk to them, and you can't do it like this. Jensen's already seen your ass, and I already want to put a bullet in him for it."

That seems to jolt her, and she loosens her hold and slides down my body. When she steps back, it's then I notice she doesn't have a bra on. Her breasts sway, and her hard pebbled nipples are pressed against her shirt. "Fuck me," I groan.

I stalk over to the closet and pull out a pair of shorts. Then I go over to her drawers and start pulling them open roughly. I see her lace panties, silky nightgowns, and in the third drawer, I find her bras. I grab one, the exact shade of peach as her panties, and then walk back over to her.

She's trembling, and I drop to the carpet in front of her. "Here, put your leg in here."

She does as I ask and steps into her shorts. When she tries to pull them up, I wave her hands away. "I want to do this. Let me take care of you."

She sighs heavily and lets me pull the shorts up her thighs and onto her hips. I raise up and look into her eyes. "I'm going to put your bra on," I tell her matter-of-factly. It's then I know how messed up she is when she merely nods her head. I try not to look at her large, rounded breasts or ignore the fact that her nipples are a darker shade of pink than the lacy bra I'm covering them with. She's perfection in every form, and it's fucking painful to touch her, but not really touch her. When this is over, and this terrible night is nothing but a memory, nothing is going to be able to stop me from having her.

8

SIERRA

I can't believe that after the night I had, all I can think about is how good it is to be sitting next to Evan with his arm around me. He hasn't let me go. He sat with me as I answered all the policeman's questions. And he held me even tighter when they told me they caught the guy, and he claimed he was my boyfriend. They showed me his picture, and I recognize him as a man that comes into the library. He had asked me out, but after I turned him down, he never asked again, and I thought it wasn't a big deal. However, now I'm finding out it was definitely a big deal to him. The police have already taken him in and have searched his house. He had a shrine set up of pictures of me that really freaked me out, until Evan told me that nothing or no one is going to hurt me.

When exhaustion started to set in, Evan is the

one that told the police I needed to rest and walked them to the door.

I can't take my eyes off him as he locks the door and sets the alarm. "Are you leaving?"

He shakes his head. "There's no way I could leave you now."

I breathe a sigh of relief, and my eyes well up with tears.

He rushes to me and gathers me into his arms. "You're okay. I'm not going to let anything happen to you. I'm so sorry, Sierra. I shouldn't have left..."

I pull back. "This is not your fault."

Guilt is all over his face. "I was going home to shower and grab clothes and then I was coming back, but I wasn't fast enough."

"Yes you were," I tell him. "You got here before I got hurt. You're here now."

He lays his cheek on the top of my head. "Please don't ask me to leave. Not tonight. I just need to hold you. That's it. I can move my truck if you're worried about what the neighbors think. Whatever, just don't ask me to leave."

I grab his hand and pull it over my heart to my chest. I raise my eyes and look into his. "Stay with me."

He nods, and I know he's not understanding what I'm asking him. I move his hand to cover my breast. "I want you to stay with me."

He's shaking his head but at the same time his

hand squeezes my breast. As if he just realizes what he's done, he tries to pull back, but I don't let him. "Sierra, I want you and I'm going to have you, but not like this, not after what you've been through tonight."

"No, I need you, Evan. Tonight. Please?"

I know it sounds like I'm begging him, but I don't care.

"Sierra…"

I release his hand and wrap my arms around his neck. It's the first time I've made the first move, but I don't care. Not anymore. I'm still scared. Scared that this won't last, scared I'm going to get hurt, but I'm even more scared at the thought I won't ever have this chance again. The need to have him— tonight—is strong, and I don't want to resist it.

"Please, Evan. I want you to be my first."

He groans. "Fuck, baby." His hips buck under- neath me. "You can't say stuff like that."

I grip his shoulders. "But it's true. I've dreamed about it. I've always thought you would be my first."

His jaw is tense. "Are you sure? It doesn't have to be tonight. I can be your first tomorrow, or the next day. I don't want to take advantage."

I untangle my arms and legs from him and stand up. He's already seen me almost naked, and maybe it's everything I've experienced tonight, but I'm not even self-conscious or nervous. I pull down my shorts and then pull the hem of my shirt over my head. I reach behind me and undo my bra and let it fall from my arms to the floor. Taking a deep breath, I put a finger in each side of my panties and pull them down, kicking them to the side. I'm naked, and he's staring at me. His eyes burn a path down my body and up again. His eyes have gone three shades darker, and he's not even trying to hide the desire on his face. He stands up, and the rough texture of his jeans scratch across my thighs he's so close. "This won't just be tonight, Sierra. Once with you will not be enough. A hundred, fuck a thousand times won't be enough."

I put my hand in his and pull him to the bedroom. We walk in unison, and as soon as we get beside the bed, he's stripping his clothes off. His manhood is hard, poking straight out, and I want to drop to my knees to get a closer look. But I can't. He's got his arms around me, laying me back on the bed before I can get my hands on him.

Evan

SHE'S PERFECTION. She's laid back, her legs spread, and her pussy is already glistening for me. I lick my lips, knowing that tonight I'm going to taste every inch of her. My hands slide up the inside of her legs, pushing them wider, opening her up for me.

HOPE FORD

I knead her soft thighs with my hands and look up at her. "I don't have any protection with me."

Even though that's the case, I can still make sure we both get off.

"Are you clean?"

I nod. It's been a long time for me, and I've been tested since. "Yeah, I'm clean."

She nods, lifting her legs and wrapping them around my waist, pulling me closer to her. My cock is hard, jutting out between my legs between us, and it rubs right across her mound. She lifts her hips to meet me, and I groan.

"What about babies?" I ask her, and the thought of her round with my baby doesn't scare me in the least.

But she's shaking her head. 'It's not the right time."

I don't even try to hide my disappointment or question what I'm thinking. I wrap my hand around the base of my cock and stroke it through her wet, swollen folds. She moans when I hit her clit, and so I stay there, circling her bundle of nerves. I need to make this good for her, but I also need to last. I pull my hips back and lean down to put my tongue on her clit. Her hips gyrate underneath me, and I suckle her until she's moaning my name. She's responsive to every touch, every lick, every command, and I know it's going to be explosive when I finally get inside her.

She moves her hips back and forth, her hands gripping my hair, and only seconds go by before she's tense and an orgasm rages through her. Kissing up her body, I lick and taste her, circling her nipples as she wraps her legs around my waist. My cock finds her wet, needy core, and I slide along her swollen lips.

"Please, Evan. I need you. I need this."

Unable to resist her, I angle my hips and slide into her slowly. She's gripping me tightly, but I push on.

"Look at me, baby. I need you to look at me."

She unclenches her eyes and is staring up at me in shock. I know as soon as I'm about to take her virginity from her, and in one fluid motion, I push through and don't stop until I've bottomed out inside her. We both moan, loud and low. Fuck it feels good.

When her hips start to move, I start to thrust in and out of her. Her orgasm from earlier has left her feeling sensitive, and she's pulsating all around me. "I need to come."

She nods and groans as I plow back into her, harder.

"Yes."

"I don't know if I can pull out."

Her legs tighten around me. "Don't. I want to feel it all. Give this to me, please Evan."

Her asking me for my cum is my undoing. "Come with me, baby."

And I come as she bears down on me, sucking me in and not letting me go. "Yes," I groan.

I pull out and climb off the bed backwards. Walking into the bathroom, I'm already regretting what I've done. I clean up and then walk out to her and help her do the same. "I'm sorry," I tell her with shame.

She pulls the sheet up to cover her body. "Sorry for what?"

She looks like she's on the verge of tears, and I sit down on the bed next to her. My stupid cock isn't cooperating because already I'm getting hard again. "I'm sorry, I was so rough. I was quick."

She snorts and then covers her face. "I came. Twice, Evan. I mean, were you going for a record or something?"

I shake my head. "I just wanted it to be good for you."

She pulls me to lie down with her and lays her head on my chest. "It was good. But don't worry. We have all night if you're wanting to make it up to me."

I can feel her smiling on my chest, and I run my hands up and down her bare back. I was right. One time will not be enough with her. I'm thinking forever won't be either.

EPILOGUE
SIERRA

One Month Later

FOR THE PAST MONTH, I'VE BEEN WAKING UP IN Evan McCarthy's arms. I wanted one night and the one night turned into a week... then a month. We're together all the time except for when we're at work, and even though the stalker had been caught, Evan still drives me to work each day and picks me up. And then most nights, he stays at my house with me. We've gotten closer and closer, and I've loved it, but there's something weighing on the back of my mind. Like this is just too good to last.

I'm at the house since it was a half day for me and Evan dropped me off so he could go to a doctor's appointment. When my phone rings, I answer it without looking at the caller ID. "Hello."

"Hello. May I speak to Evan McCarthy, please?"

I pull the phone back and look at it and then put it to my ear again. "Uh, no I'm sorry he isn't here. May I ask who's calling?" Whoever it is sounds pretty official.

"Yes. This is Commander Jamison. I got your number from Evan's brother when I called his office. He thought Evan might be there. Can you please tell him I'm trying to track him down and have him call me?"

I'm nodding into the phone, and my stomach sinks at the same time. "Yes. I'll tell him."

The phone clicks in my ear, and I walk over to the couch and drop into it.

I don't know how much time passes, and Evan walks into my house, whistling.

He spots me and stops, and I try to hide the pain on my face. He drops down in front of me. "What's wrong?"

I shake my head. "What did the doctor say?"

His smile when he first walked in lessens a little but he still tells me, "All my tests were good. They said I'll be able to return to all normal activities soon."

I smile, but I know it doesn't quite reach my eyes. Don't get me wrong, I want him well. I hate the pain he's gone through with the vertigo, but I also don't want him to leave. "That's so great, Evan. I'm so happy for you."

I pull him in for a hug to hide my face. He can always read me, sometimes knowing what I'm feeling before I even tell him, and I don't want to bring him down. I want him happy.

His arms tighten around me. "What is it?"

"No—"

But before I can get "nothing" out, he interrupts me. "Don't say nothing. There's something wrong. Tell me."

I pull away and stand up, sliding around him to put some distance between us. "Nothing is wrong. Oh yeah, your commander called. He wants you to call him back."

He's quiet for a minute, and I start to walk out of the room, but he follows me. I think I can hold it together until he puts his hands on my shoulders to stop me. It's then that the floodgates open, and tears are pouring down my face.

I turn in his arms and plaster myself to him. I can't imagine losing him. Not now. And knowing he's okay, that he can return to all his duties, I know he's probably going to leave me.

He lets me cry, and when I start to calm down, he just holds me tighter. "Tell me what it is. I can't fix it if you don't tell me."

"It's nothing. I'm happy you're okay. I'm happy

you can go back to your duties...." I trail off, and that's when it clicks.

"You think I'm going back to the Army?"

I shrug my shoulders, not wanting to even say it out loud.

He pulls back enough to look at me. He takes the pad of his thumb and wipes the tears off my cheeks. "Baby, a month and a half ago, I would have gone back in an instant, but now, knowing you, feeling what we have together, I won't leave you. I can't."

"But you love the Army. That's what you've always wanted to do."

He shakes his head. "And I did it. I served my country, and I did it with pride. But I love you, Sierra. I won't leave you. I promised you I wouldn't hurt you and I won't."

"You love me?" I ask in shock.

"Fuck, isn't it obvious? I'm obsessed with you."

Elation and guilt build at the same time. "But I don't want to hold you back."

He laughs and shakes his head. "You would never hold me back. It's my decision. I have vertigo, yes, the symptoms are less, and I can resume working out and running, but I'm not cleared for duty. I'm here to stay, Sierra. I want to build a life with you."

I kiss his chest, right over his heart and whisper

up to him with emotion thick in my voice. "I'd like that too. I love you, Evan."

Evan

SHE DOESN'T EVEN KNOW. She has no clue that my life starts and ends with her. She has become my everything in such a short amount of time. We may not have gotten together in high school, but now, it's like perfect timing because we fit together perfectly. "I love you more," I tell her before lifting her up and carrying her to the bedroom. I'm insatiable when it comes to her. I can't get enough.

I slide my hands down the front of her shorts, and she's already soaked for me. I strip us both from the waist down because I have to have her and can't wait another second.

She slides her hips back. "We can't. Not without anything. Not unless you want a little Evan popping out in nine months."

"Fuck," I grunt as my hips thrust against her.

I kiss her, fitting my body between her legs, my cock already leaking precum. Just the thought of getting her pregnant is enough to make me come right now. "I'm fine with that."

Her eyes grow wide. "Evan!"

I shrug and slide my cock along her slit, begging

for entrance. "What? I am. We're going to get married and have babies anyway."

"Evan..."

I grab my cock and stroke it along her clit. "It's up to you, baby. I can stop if you want me to."

She moans, and I leak more cum, our juices mixing together. "Don't you dare stop, Evan McCarthy."

I plunge into her hot depths and fuck, it feels like home. "I won't, baby. I'll never stop."

EPILOGUE 2

VIOLET

I'M A GENIUS, IF I DO SAY SO MYSELF. I'M LOOKING around my little diner, and seeing the couples in the room all happy and enjoying their life makes me smile. I've helped the majority of them get together, and I swear I should open a matchmaking company. I could make a killing.

Evan and Sierra are sitting in the corner, and they can't keep their hands off each other. I'm sure there's going to be an announcement soon about upcoming nuptials, and I'm sure I'll get to be a bridesmaid... again.

Without thinking about it, I put my hand in the front pocket of my jeans and run my fingers across the smooth metal ring that I carry there every day. It's great seeing all the people of Whiskey Run finding love, it really is. But there's a part of me that is bothered that I'll never have that. I won't ever go to sleep in my husband's arms or wake up with him next to me. No, as a matter of fact, I probably won't even be married much longer.

I turn and wipe down the counter, not wanting Sierra to see me upset. She knows a little about things. Well, she at least knows I'm married, but I never told her the details. I couldn't. I am so embarrassed; I feel my face heat just thinking about it.

The bell over the door chimes, and I turn with a smile plastered to my face, ready to welcome the newcomer. But instantly my smile drops because in walks Josh Chambers, the running back for the Jasper Eagles. I drop the cloth in my hand, and all the blood drains from my face. I grip the edge of the counter to try and stay upright.

He looks around the diner before his gaze finally lands on mine. There's a hush in the diner. Everyone knows who he is. He's a football legend. The youngest player to ever had made it to the big game and score the winning touchdown. Little Tommy, who's in one of the booths, rushes toward him. "Mr. Chambers, can I have your autograph?"

Tommy's mom is behind him with a pen and napkin, and Josh takes it, signing his name but never taking his eyes off me. I'm about to bolt. I know it, and I'm sure he does too. He smiles for the kid, pats him on the head, and walks toward me.

"Hello, Mrs. Chambers."

I wince when he calls me by my married name.

I look around the diner, and sure enough everyone is hanging on every word.

"What are you doing here?" I ask him and then hold my breath. He must have finally received the copy of the divorce papers. But that doesn't explain why he's here. All he had to do is sign them and send them back. I put that in the note.

He cages me in, one hand on each side of me. "Why do you think I'm here?" he asks softly. His tone doesn't match his stance. He's rigid, and I can almost feel the electricity raging through his body. It was the same way the night I met him. Just being next to him is like being next to a live wire.

I shrug, not answering him.

There's a hush in the diner, and I know without a shadow of a doubt that this is going to be spread all over Whiskey Run before sunrise. Everyone in town will know about legend Josh Chambers being in the diner to talk to me. But that's the least of my problems.

I reach out to put my hands at his waist and pull back instantly. I was going to push him away, but I know I can't touch him. I know what happens when I do.

"Is everything okay, Violet?"

I look over Josh's shoulder, and Sierra and Evan are standing behind him. Josh grabs my hand and turns to face them. "Yeah, everything is fine. I just came to talk to my wife."

There's a gasp in the restaurant, and everyone is obviously shocked. But not Sierra—no, she's looking at me with a smug look on her face. She may not have known the whole story, but she saw the marriage certificate; she knew who I was married to. Evan steps in front of Sierra, no doubt able to feel the waves of testosterone coming off Josh. I swear I wouldn't be surprised if he took out a full-page ad in the Whiskey Run Gazette telling everyone I am his wife. I mean, he might as well for how he's acting.

I step around him. "Evan, I'm fine. Thanks." And then I turn back to Josh. "I sent you the divorce papers. All you had to do was sign them and send them back. That's it."

He grunts, and coming from him, it's more like a growl. I've seen three hundred pound men scared of him but not me. No, I'm not scared in the least. At least not physically.

It's like I can hear his jaw cracking when he says, "I'm not signing the damn papers."

I blink. Once, then again. "What do you mean you're not signing the papers? That's the only way to end the marriage."

He wraps his big hand around my neck and pulls me in close. "I'm not signing the papers because you're my wife... and I'm keeping you."

I shake my head. "What did you just say?"

He repeats himself, and I heard him right the

first time, but he enunciates each word. "Because. You're. My. Wife. And. I'm. Keeping. You."

And without any warning at all, he leans down and presses his lips to mine. The kiss is equivalent to every explicit dream I've had since the night I married him. I have no control when he looks at me, touches me, or kisses me, and even months later, it still remains the same. The man can kiss like nobody's business.

He plays dirty. I know this about him. He seduced me at his house in Jasper months ago. He's made grown men cry on the football field. He's tough and gruff and never loses, so I shouldn't be surprised that he didn't like my letter asking for a divorce. But surely, he'll come to his senses. He's a famous football player who's in his prime. I'm a diner owner from a small town who's six years older than him. Surely, he'll realize I'm not what he wants, not what he needs.

I wrench my lips from his, and I'm breathing heavily as if I've been running a race instead of kissing my husband.

I turn to walk away, and he grabs my hand. "No way, darling. You've escaped me once but not again. Where you go, I go."

He walks with me to the back of the diner, and as soon as the swinging door shuts I hear half the town sitting in my diner all start talking at once.

I walk out the back door and try to figure out how I'm going to get myself out of this mess.

Get Violet and Josh's story here. Get Seduced now.
mybook.to/SeducedHopeFord

Want to peek into Evan and Sierra's
happily ever after?
It's a good one.
Keep reading for the bonus epilogue.

BONUS EPILOGUE

EVAN

Nine Months Later

I thought boot camp was the hardest thing I've ever had to do. It was mentally and physically grueling, and I thought I wouldn't survive it. But come to find out, it's nothing compared to watching my wife, the woman I love, give birth.

She's been in labor for almost twenty-four hours, and I'm about to lose my mind. She's in so much pain, and as soon as the doctor walks into the room, I charge toward him. "She can't keep this up. It's been twenty-four hours, doc. Something needs to happen, and it needs to be now."

The doctor, who has always been patient and kind even when Sierra and I have asked a gazillion questions, looks worried. He walks toward Sierra and simply put, she looks haggard. She can barely lift her head she's so tired. She's still the most beautiful woman I've ever seen, but she's tired.

She tries to smile. "Hey, Doc. Sorry about my husband, he's a worrywart."

She tries to joke, but to me it's no joking matter. I crowd the doctor and am quiet while he's examining her, but when his face loses a little color and gets even more of a worried look, I have to say something. "So what are we going to do?"

I have my hands crossed on my chest because I know if I don't, I'm going to put my hands on him, and that's not going to do anything but upset Sierra. And even though she's used to my overpowering controlling ways, she doesn't need to deal with it right now. That's the only thing that's stopping me from putting my fist into the doctor's face right now.

He blows out a breath and talks in his calming voice. "We are going to have to do an emergency C-section. She's not dilating, and the baby needs to come out." He turns to Sierra, and I grab on to the edge of the bed before I fall out into the floor. I've read up on all this baby delivering shit. I've watched the movies, gone to the class, did it all. I've also read about all the things that can go wrong. "Not dilating" and "baby needs to come out" tells me that I need to be worried. My wife is about to have surgery.

"Doctor, is there any other way?"

"No. I'm afraid there's not. But you shouldn't worry. Your wife is strong, she can handle this."

Twenty-four hours ago I would have agreed with him, but now I'm not so sure. She's weak and tired, and the fight has gone out of her.

"Sierra, honey, look at me. I'm going to be right there with you, okay?"

"Actually," the doctor interrupts, and I give him a death stare.

"What? What is it now?"

He clears his throat. "It's too late to do an epidural. We will have to put her under, and unfortunately it's hospital policy that no one can be in there."

"The fuck I can't," I boom loud enough to rattle the glass of the windows.

"Evan. Evan. Look at me," Sierra says, holding her hand out to me. "I'll be back before you know it."

"I can't," I tell her, and a tear rolls down my cheek. I have no shame. I don't care if I'm a grown fucking man, I can't let my wife do this on her own. I can't.

"Everything is going to be fine. I'm going to have the baby, and I'll be out here in an hour, and we'll all be together."

The buzzing of the machine gets louder, and I know it's my son right now that needs help. "I love you." I bend down and kiss her, my tears falling onto her face as she's kissing me back.

"I love you too. We'll be back soon. I promise," she says, and they wheel her down the hallway. I hold her hand the whole way until we get to the door that I'm not allowed past.

A nurse takes pity on me. "I'll keep you updated."

I nod but keep my eyes on Sierra. I squeeze her hand and let her go, hollering after her, "I love you, Sierra."

I go back to the room and pace. I've never felt so helpless in my life. If anything happens to her or our son, I don't know what I'll do. The anguish inside me guts me. I've seen my brothers in arms shot. I've seen innocent people hurt. I've been shot and stabbed, and the list goes on. But none of it even comes close to how I feel right now.

I sit down in my chair and put my face in my hands. I plead with the man above to make sure my family is all right. I don't know how much time goes by, but when the door opens, I bound from my seat. It's the nurse that went with Sierra, and she's holding a baby. "Here you go. I'd like you to meet your son."

I hold my hands out to take him. "Where's my wife?" I demand.

"She's in recovery. We'll bring her in as soon as she wakes up."

I look down at the little guy in my arms. He's snuggled tightly in a blanket and sleeping peacefully. I touch my finger to his fat little cheek, and he opens his eyes. He's staring back at me and it's his momma's blue eyes that are staring back at me. Looking at him literally takes my breath away. I sit down in the chair and snuggle him close. "Hey, little guy. I'm your daddy. Your momma and I have been waiting to meet you."

I swear he smiles, but I know other people would tell me it's gas. We sit like that for a while, content just looking at each other.

When the door opens again, I can't jump up like I did before, but I do get up and walk over to the bed as they move my wife into place. She's groggy and still in and out of it. "Hey, baby. You did good."

She smiles and then opens her eyes. "I love you" is the first thing she says, and I'm crying again.

"I love you too. I have someone here you may want to meet."

Her eyes snap open, and she looks at the bundle in my arms. I lay him down onto her chest, and mother and son look at each other in awe. I put a hand on each of them because right now, I can't ever imagine letting either one of them out of my sight again. The hour or so they were gone was the longest of my life, and I never want to go through anything like it again.

I push the hair off her face. "You look beautiful, Momma."

She laughs. "Oh, you're a good man, Evan McCarthy."

I nod my head at our son. "So what are we going to call him?"

We've thrown around a bunch of names, but never made a decision. "EJ," she says without even hesitating.

"EJ?"

"Yeah, short for Evan McCarthy Junior."

My heart clutches in my chest, and the tears start to well again. "Fuck, woman, you're killing me today."

She tsks at me. "No cussing in front of EJ."

I nod my head and lean down to kiss EJ on the head, and then I kiss my wife on the lips. "Thank you."

She smiles and no doubt already knows the answer but asks anyway. "For what?"

I put my hand at her neck. "For loving me in high school. For sending me care packages when I was gone. For giving me a chance. For loving me now. For being my wife and making me a father. I love you, baby."

She turns her head and kisses my palm. "I love you more."

FREE BOOKS

Want FREE BOOKS?
Go to www.authorhopeford.com/freebies

JOIN ME!

JOIN MY NEWSLETTER & READERS GROUP

www.AuthorHopeFord.com/Subscribe

JOIN MY READERS GROUP ON FACEBOOK

www.FB.com/groups/hopeford

Find Hope Ford at www.authorhopeford.com

ABOUT THE AUTHOR

USA Today Bestselling Author Hope Ford writes short, steamy, sweet romances. She loves tattooed, alpha men, instant love stories, and ALWAYS happily ever afters. She has over 100 books and they are all available on Amazon.

To find me on Pinterest, Instagram, Facebook, Goodreads, and more:

www.AuthorHopeFord.com/follow-me

Printed in Great Britain
by Amazon

17310295R00055

Printed in Great Britain
by Amazon

60532415R10122